FINDIN' OUT

REAL ESTATE RESCUE COZY MYSTERIES, BOOK 3

PATTI BENNING

D1607629

SUMMER PRESCOTT BOOKS PUBLISHING

CHAPTER ONE

Summer droned on. It had never felt quite so long to her before, but that could have been because Flora Abner had spent her previous summers— all the seasons, really—in the state of constant busyness that came from having a full-time office job along with maintaining a decent social life, all while living in the middle of Chicago.

Things were slower here, in Warbler, Kentucky. She suspected that would be true even if she went into an office from nine to five, but focusing each of her long days on fixing up the house she intended to flip in less than two years only highlighted the difference. Her days were still full, but they weren't monotonous. She was still busy, but that frantic pace was nonexistent.

She found herself pausing sometimes to enjoy the small things, things she had never even taken the time to notice before. Like right now. It was a hot day in the middle of the week. The insects were droning from the shade in the forest, and she and two of her closest friends were sweltering in the sunlight as they painted a fresh coat of white paint on the siding they had stripped and sanded just the day before. Well, she and Grady were painting. Violet was standing in the shade on the porch, typing out a text message on her phone before she left.

It shouldn't have been fun. It was *hot* out, the sort of heat that gave her a dehydration headache if she wasn't drinking from her water bottle almost constantly, and despite the sunscreen she had applied an hour ago, she would probably end the day with at least a minor sunburn on her shoulders. A bee kept buzzing around her head, and her shirt stuck to her sweaty lower back. But despite all of that, she was happy. It was a low hum of contentment in her chest, a feeling of everything being right with the world. Sure, it was hard work, and Grady had already dripped some of the white paint into her hair from where he was working on the ladder to paint the upper story siding, but she wouldn't change a thing.

Well, maybe one thing.

"Are you sure you have to go?" she asked as she set her paintbrush down on a tray beside the open can of paint and pulled her shirt away from her back. Maybe she should check the prices on aboveground pools. It was an unnecessary expense and seemed like a lot of work to maintain, but it would be one-hundred percent worth it if she could go for a swim when the weather was like this.

"I'm sorry," Violet said, the regret in her voice sounding genuine. "Missy's got a fever, and I just can't ask my employees to work when they're sick, especially not around the food and drinks."

Violet owned the best coffee store in town, a small corner building with a violently purple interior called Violet Delights. It was a quirky place, but then, Violet was a quirky person, and even the more conservative townsfolk seemed too enamored by the drinks she served to care about the odd decor inside.

"It's okay," Flora said. She didn't want her friend to feel bad. "I get it. I hope she feels better. Being sick is no fun."

"We're only doing one side of the house, anyway," Grady said from his place up on the ladder. "There will be plenty left to do this weekend."

A car drove past them on the dirt road in front of Flora's house. She waved at it without paying much attention—it was one of the habits she had picked up over the past couple of months. Waving at everyone who drove by in Chicago would have led to her arm falling off. Here, on a dirt road a couple of miles away from a tiny town, chances were that whoever was driving by was someone she would run into regularly. Waving at the occasional passerby was only polite.

"I can come out on Saturday," Violet offered as she stuffed her phone into her purse. "I bet Sydney is available too. We can help with the siding for a few hours, then watch a movie or something."

"Sounds good," Flora said. She made to give her friend a brief hug as she came down the stairs, but decided against it at the last moment, since she had a smear of wet paint on her wrist and possibly more splatters elsewhere on her body, and Violet had already changed out of her painting clothes. Instead, she just waved. "I'll probably swing by the coffee shop tomorrow. Watch out for the garbage truck on your way out. Pickup usually happens around this time, and he tends to park in the middle of the road."

"I'll keep an eye out. See you, Flora. See you, Grady."

Grady waved at her with the paintbrush, and Flora watched as Violet pulled out of the driveway and started down the road. It was a bummer the other woman had to leave early, but at least Grady was still here to keep her company. The three of them had become closer over the past couple of weeks, and though Grady and Violet didn't exactly hang out with each other without Flora around, they were all comfortable and friendly with each other. Sydney, the man around Violet's age who worked at the feed store and had helped them catch a killer the month before, was another new addition to Flora's slowly growing circle of friends. She had even more acquaintances, all people Violet had introduced her to, and no longer felt quite as isolated here as she had when she first moved in.

"Want to take a break and have some lemonade?" she called up to Grady when she turned back to the house.

5

"We've still got all afternoon to finish, and this heat is killing me."

"It's not all that bad out here," he replied. "But all right. I could use something cold to drink."

He left the can of paint he was using loosely covered at the top of the ladder and climbed down. At the bottom of it, he reached up to shove his brown hair away from his eyes, and she found her eyes lingering on the muscles of his arm for a moment before the sound of tires on gravel grabbed her attention.

A glance down the road confirmed that the garbage truck had indeed turned onto her street. The turn off from the main road was half a mile down, and her house was the first one on the road. Past her were the Yorks, an older couple that she genuinely liked, even if Beth could be a little irritating sometimes, and past them, out of sight beyond a curve and a lot of trees, were a handful of other houses. She'd met most of the other people who lived on her dirt road by now, but only in passing. The Yorks were easily the neighbors she knew the best.

"I'm going to go grab some lemonade for Cameron too," she told Grady as she hurried toward the front door. "If he gets here before I come out, tell him to wait, would you?"

"Sure," Grady said.

Cameron was a sort-of friend of his—the two had gone to school together but had lost touch after graduating, despite both having lived in the same small town all their lives. She hadn't known of the connection until Grady coincidentally stopped by one day during the weekly garbage pickup and the two started talking. Warbler was filled with small connections like that. It seemed quaint and unexpected to her, but she had a feeling if she had lived here her whole life, it would just feel suffocating.

She went into the house, closing the door behind her quickly while blocking the exit with her legs. Amaretto, her fluffy, white Persian cat, had gotten out once weeks ago, and had apparently liked the experience enough that she was determined to repeat it. Flora was even more determined not to let her cat become coyote food, and so far, it was a battle she was winning.

The interior the house was dark and somewhat cool. The ancient window air conditioner in the living room could only beat back the heat if she kept the curtains drawn, and it had nothing on the frigid, industrial-style air conditioners most of the modern buildings in Chicago boasted, but it was still a lot better than roasting in the sun.

Sadly, the living room was the only room in the house that benefited from the unit, and the temperature increased steadily as she walked down the hall to the kitchen. She appreciated the blast of cold air as she pulled the fridge open and took out the pitcher of lemonade. It was from a powdered mix, something Beth had served her once when she visited, and she had liked well enough to seek it out at the grocery store herself. Maybe it wasn't as healthy as the real thing, but it was a lot easier to make, and it hit the spot like nothing else did on sweltering days like today.

She poured three tall glasses of the lemonade and carried them back outside, careful not to spill any as she blocked Amaretto from the door again. Cameron's garbage truck was parked in the middle of the road in front of her house, and by the looks of it, he had already emptied the dumpster. He and Grady were chatting as she approached with the lemonade. She handed a glass over to each of them, then took a sip of her own. It was still ice cold from the fridge. Perfect.

"Thanks," Cameron said. "I don't mind what I do, but it's miserable on days like today. Even those insulated water bottles can't keep anything cold for long."

They chatted for a minute, until he had finished the drink and handed the glass back. She and Grady stepped away from the truck as it started moving. Flora waved as it pulled away, then kept waving when she saw Beth on the road farther up. The older woman looked like she was just leaving her house to go on a walk with her Basset hound, Sammy. They were heading down the road away from Flora's house, probably because there were more trees and thus more shade that way. Beth waved back, then turned away and started ambling along the road. Flora watched as the garbage truck pulled up in front of the Yorks' house, then turned back to Grady.

"Back to work?"

"Yep." He eyed the front of the house. "It's already looking better. A new coat of paint makes a lot of difference."

"So does the roof. Not that I don't appreciate your help with the tarp, but it's nice to have the work finally done."

The roofing company had finished just last week. It had been an annoying project, with a lot of noise and mess, but now the old house had a brand-new roof.

"You won't hardly be able to recognize the place when you're done with it," he said as he started climbing back up the ladder. Flora smiled and grabbed her own paintbrush. She could hardly wait to compare the before and after pictures of this place when she was finally done. It really was going to be unrecognizable.

They fell into an easy silence as they worked, only occasionally talking when one of them made a comment about the bugs, or an apology from Grady when he dripped more paint down that just barely missed her. The day was peaceful and quiet other than for the sound of the insects, and Flora got lost in thought as she worked.

At least, until maybe ten minutes later, when a gunshot echoed out over the trees.

She jolted and looked around, but it was impossible to tell where the sound had come from. It had happened a couple of times before, and she knew it was just a part of living in the country, where people occasionally had to kill vermin or went hunting, but it startled her every time, and she had never heard one that sounded so close before.

"You all right?" Grady asked from above, seeming to have noticed her discomfort.

"Yeah, just surprised," she admitted.

"It was probably just—"

He broke off midsentence because that was when the screaming started.

CHAPTER TWO

Flora and Grady's eyes met for a second, then he rushed down the ladder, dropping his paintbrush in his haste. Flora ran out into the road, intending to head in the direction of the screams, which seemed to be coming from past Beth's house, but Grady said, "The truck'll be faster, and we can take someone to the hospital if we need to."

He was right. She changed direction and climbed into the passenger seat of his truck, which was parked in what had become its normal spot behind hers. He got into the driver's side and grabbed the keys out of the cup holder. No sooner had the truck roared to life than he jerked it into reverse and backed onto the road before putting it in drive and spitting up gravel as he hurried in the direction the screams were coming from.

The truck rattled past Beth's house and into the shade of the trees that lined the road beyond it. They approached the curve in the road a little too fast, and Grady had to slam on the brakes when they rounded it to see Beth and her dog standing in the road. Flora had been in too much of a hurry to remember to put her seatbelt on, and she threw out her hands to catch herself on the dashboard. Her palms hit it with enough force to hurt. She ignored it and rolled down her window as Grady eased the truck alongside the older woman. Beth's eyes were wide and panicked, and Sammy was barking, which was unusual for the usually calm dog.

"What happened?" Flora asked.

"I don't know!" Beth said. "Sammy and I were walking, and we heard a gun go off, then someone started screaming. It sounds like it's coming from the Wolperts' place."

Beth looked like she wanted to help, and Flora debated having her get in the truck, but Grady's truck only had two doors and the back seat was cramped. They didn't have time for Flora to climb back there and for the older woman to climb into the front.

"Go back to your house, and be ready to direct an ambulance this way," she said instead. "We'll go see what happened, and we'll call nine-one-one if we need to."

With that, Grady pressed the gas pedal down again, and they took off. Flora knew who the Wolperts were —a couple about her own age, who owned the next house past the curve in the road. She'd only spoken to them twice, once when they came over to introduce themselves and once when she had joined Beth for a walk and the couple were outside doing some yard work. They seemed nice enough, if busy. Natalie worked in a town about half an hour away as a nurse, and Spencer worked from home at a job that seemed to keep him tied to his computer all day.

As soon as they rounded the curve, Flora knew Beth's guess about where the shot had come from was right. Two people were in the Wolperts' yard. One was lying on his back in the grass, too still, and the other was kneeling next to him, her hands on his chest. Grady pulled the truck right into the grass, and both of them got out. Flora hurried over to the people in

PATTI BENNING

the yard. She recognized them as Natalie and Spencer right away. Natalie was putting pressure on a wound in his chest, though from the amount of blood on her hands and his clothes, Flora wasn't sure how much good it was doing.

"What happened?" she gasped as she dropped to her knees next to them.

"I don't know," Natalie said. She didn't even seem to recognize Flora in her panic. "I was in the back when I heard what sounded like a gun go off, and when I came around to the front to see what had happened, I saw him in the grass. Spencer? Spencer, can you hear me?"

The man remained motionless. Flora couldn't tell if he was breathing. "Did you call the police?" she asked. Natalie shook her head. Flora stood up and pulled her cell phone out of her back pocket. She tossed it to Grady, who immediately turned the screen on to make the call, and then she ran back to Grady's truck. She knew he kept some extra supplies in there, including a folded blanket on the back seat, and that was what she grabbed before running back to where Natalie was kneeling next to Spencer.

They used the blanket to try to put pressure on the wound and stem the bleeding, but Flora was beginning to think it was too late. The bleeding seemed to be slowing, but no matter how carefully she watched, Spencer didn't seem to be breathing. She kept her mouth shut, though. Natalie was already crying, and Flora didn't need to make things worse.

Grady let them know the police and paramedics were on their way, but it seemed like an awfully long time before she heard the sirens approaching. Grady moved his truck so the ambulance would have the space it needed to pull up. A police cruiser pulled into the driveway as the ambulance pulled onto the grass. As paramedics rushed out, Flora rose to her feet and backed away, shaking. Grady put a hand on her shoulder and squeezed it in an attempt to give her some comfort.

Natalie stood back as the paramedics got to work on her husband, but Flora found that she couldn't watch. A part of her already knew that it was too late. Instead, her gaze found Officer Hendricks, who was speaking into his police radio. His gaze lingered on her and Grady. She didn't see any outright suspicion in it, but she knew he had to be wondering how they were involved *this* time. Grady's brother was a known troublemaker and felon, and she was a newcomer from a big city. The two of them had been involved with more than one murder since Flora moved here, and even though none of it had been their *fault*, she knew that at some point, it would start looking bad.

Her excuse of just having really, really bad luck was an honest one, but she wasn't sure if Officer Hendricks would accept it this time.

CHAPTER THREE

It was getting dark by the time Flora made it back home. She pulled into the driveway in her own truck, which she had taken into town when she and Grady went in to give a formal statement at the police station and sat in the driver's seat for a moment. Idly, she thought that the paint was probably ruined by now. Neither she nor Grady had taken the time to close the cans or clean the brushes before they left. It didn't matter.

A man was dead.

Her *neighbor*, Spencer Wolpert, was dead.

She hadn't known him well, but it didn't make the knowledge any less shocking. He had been declared

19

dead at the hospital, and even though she had expected it, the news had still shaken her.

Her neighbor. Shot to death outside his house.

It wasn't as if the same thing didn't happen in Chicago, but it had always felt distant to her, there. It was something that happened in the bad parts of town —gang violence, that never really touched her or the people she knew.

This? It could have been her, or Beth. It felt so much more real here, in the small town of Warbler, right on the very street she lived on.

She took a deep breath and got out of the truck. Officer Hendricks hadn't told them much, but she suspected he didn't have any real leads yet. There weren't any security cameras out here, besides the ones she had, which were focused on her own property. No one had seen what happened, or at least, no one was admitting they had seen it. Flora had no idea if someone had targeted Spencer specifically, or if it had been a random act of violence.

There wasn't anything she could do, except keep her eyes open and wait for someone to come forward, or for the police to find forensic evidence that would lead them to the culprit.

"Yoo-hoo! Flora!"

The shout made Flora jump and drop the keys she was taking out of her purse. At the foot of the porch steps, she turned around to see Beth hurrying down the road toward her, just recognizable in the gathering gloom. Her stomach dropped. Had something else happened?

Quickly, she stooped to grab the keys, then hurried toward Beth. "What is it?" she asked.

Beth slowed to a halt, breathing a little hard from the exertion of her jog. "I just saw that you pulled in. I wanted to talk to you, dear. Is now a good time?"

It wasn't, but not for any concrete reasons Flora could put into words. She knew she could just tell the other woman she was tired and needed some time to herself, but it seemed a little rude, and her conscience nagged at her, reminding her that Beth had known the Wolperts for years. This had to be hard for her, and her husband, Tim, wasn't always mentally *there* enough to talk to her about something like this.

So, even though she didn't exactly want to talk to Beth right now, she smiled and said, "Sure. Come on in. I've got to give Amaretto her dinner, but we can talk while she's eating."

She led Beth into her house. After greeting the cat, who had grown used to her being home most of the day and seemed to have missed her, she shut off the air conditioner, turned on the lights, and went into the kitchen, the older woman following her. She opened a can of cat food and scooped the contents into Amaretto's bowl, then gestured at the kitchen table. She and Beth sat down.

"How are you doing, dear?" Beth asked. "You were gone for quite a long time. Do the police know who fired the shot?"

"I had to wait a while to give my statement," Flora said. "The police were busy. They canvassed the area, but I don't think they found anything. Officer Hendricks couldn't tell me much, but I get the feeling they don't have any suspects yet."

Beth shook her head. "How horrible. Things like this shouldn't happen here in Warbler. My heart breaks for poor Natalie. You know, I remember when she and Spencer first moved in. It must've been five years ago now. They've had their share of problems, but they were always both so kind to Tim and me."

"Do *you* have any idea who might have shot him?" Flora asked. "You know everyone, it seems like. Did they have any enemies? Did you ever notice anything strange going on at their house?"

"Well, like I said, they were very nice people. I sometimes wondered…" She shook her head. "No, that doesn't matter now. I don't know anyone who would have done such a thing. You didn't happen to see Natalie while you were at the police station, did you? I made a casserole for her, since I'm sure the poor dear isn't in any condition to cook. I don't know if she's home yet, though, and I don't want to walk all the way to her house carrying that heavy casserole dish if she isn't."

"I can't imagine she's going back to the house tonight," Flora said. If it was her, she wouldn't want to be alone right now. "She's probably staying with family, if she has any in the area."

"If she *is* at home, I hate to think how alone she feels," Beth said. "Do you think you could give me a ride over there? We would have to stop by my house to grab the casserole, but it wouldn't take more than a few minutes. I want to check up on her."

Flora sighed. She should have known Beth was fishing for something like this. "Sure," she said.

It really wouldn't take that long, and she *was* a little worried the older woman would try to carry the casserole over to the Wolperts' house on her own. Beth seemed spry for someone her age, but Flora hated the thought of the older woman walking along the road in the dark by herself, carrying a heavy casserole dish. It seemed like a recipe for disaster, even if the disaster just ended up being a dropped casserole.

She grabbed her purse and her keys, and they made their way back out of the house. She paused to lock the front door behind her. After the shooting earlier, she wasn't taking any chances with security—and then made sure the front seat of her truck was cleared off for Beth. The older woman climbed in, and Flora got into the driver's side. With a turn of the key, the engine roared to life, and she backed out of the driveway.

Beth seemed subdued as they drove the quarter of a mile down the road to her house. She looked out the window, not saying anything as the evening landscape rolled by. Flora pulled into her driveway.

"Do you want me to come in and carry the casserole out to the truck for you?" she offered.

Beth shook her head. "I can go get it myself. I'll be right back, dear."

She patted Flora's knee and got out of the truck. Flora kept it running as she waited. It only took a minute for the older woman to reappear with the casserole dish in her hands. Flora pushed the passenger door open and accepted the dish from Beth, holding it while the older woman climbed into her seat. The casserole smelled delicious, and Flora's stomach reminded her she hadn't eaten since lunch.

Once Beth was buckled in, Flora handed the dish back to her and pulled out of the driveway, setting off down the road to the Wolperts' house. She took the curve in the road slowly, remembering how suddenly Beth seemed to appear on it earlier. She didn't drive this way down the road very often, but she made a mental note to be careful whenever she did. The last thing she wanted to do was hit someone who was out for a jog.

Flora wasn't expecting to see anyone at the Wolperts' house, so when she came around the curve and spotted a silver car in the driveway, she frowned. The car seemed familiar, but she didn't know these neighbors well enough to be certain what sort of vehicle they drove. Maybe Natalie was back at the house already.

She put her blinker on, intending to turn into the driveway. Before she could make the turn, the silver car's reverse lights came on, and it started backing up. She paused, keeping her truck sitting in the road as the vehicle pulled out of the driveway. For a moment, as it pulled out onto the road, it was facing her. She could see a woman's outline in the car, but then the vehicle's headlights came on, and it pulled forward, driving past her with a spit of gravel. She and Beth watched it go, then glanced at each other.

"That was weird," Flora said. She pulled into the driveway, but the house was dark, and there was no sign of anyone else there. "I don't think anyone's home. Do you want me to go knock on the door?"

Beth shook her head with a sigh.

"No, you were right. She must be spending the night elsewhere."

"That wasn't her car, then?" Flora asked as she reversed out of the driveway. She pulled down the road, going the same direction the silver car had been —back to Beth's house. The other vehicle was long gone, though. As she went around the curve, she saw a faint glow of red lights at the end of the road, past her house, then the car turned toward town and was gone.

"No, she drives a dark red sedan." Beth frowned. "I *have* seen that silver car before."

"Do you know who it belongs to?" Flora asked.

"I have my suspicions," the older woman said. Her lips were pressed together, and she refused to say anymore.

Flora dropped Beth back off at her house, then headed home. It had been an odd evening. She had even more questions than before but had a feeling she would be able to get the answers out of Beth if she waited long enough. She had no idea why the older woman was being so secretive right now, but she knew it wouldn't last long. If there was one thing Beth loved to do, it was to talk.

CHAPTER FOUR

Flora didn't drive past the Wolperts' house to check for Natalie again, but Beth seemed determined to keep her updated on the fact that the woman wasn't home yet. Privately, Flora thought Beth was enjoying all of this just a little too much. It was an uncharitable thought—she knew Beth was truly horrified at what had happened to Spencer—but the older woman seemed to be taking advantage of the chance to gossip about it.

Other than Violet, who asked Flora what the heck had happened, and Grady, who asked her only once if she had heard anything about the police investigation, no one approached Flora for the details of the shooting. Part of that might have been because she spent most

29

of her time over the next few days working on her house. She was stripping the old paint on the wooden siding off in preparation for this weekend, which was supposed to be sunny, warm, and the perfect weather for painting.

She always felt a little guilty asking her friends for help, but Violet, Grady, and Sydney all seemed happy to come over that Saturday and help her, in exchange for a movie night and possibly a bonfire. She spent Saturday morning making sure her house was tidy and that she had plenty of snacks and drinks, and that the fire pit was cleaned out in case they wanted to spend some time sitting around a bonfire.

Violet was the first to arrive Saturday afternoon. The coffee shop closed earlier than the feed store or the hardware shop, where Sydney and Grady worked, and as the owner, no one was going to stop Violet from leaving a little early. She seemed to be in good spirits, and after she changed into her painting clothes, the two of them spent a fun couple of hours chatting while painting the siding. Flora had a portable Bluetooth speaker, which they brought out so they could listen to music while they worked. The lingering shock of the murder was the only thing bringing

Flora's mood down. It would have been the perfect day, otherwise.

Grady and Sydney arrived within just a few minutes of each other a couple of hours later. She and Violet had made good progress on the west side of the house, and with the help from the men, they got it finished as the sun started to go down.

"It's looking good," Violet said with a low whistle as they stepped back to admire the house from an angle that allowed them to see the two finished sides. "I bet you could flip this place as it is. With a new roof and a fresh coat of paint, it looks a lot better."

"If you want me out of your hair sooner rather than later, just say it," Flora joked.

Violet grinned. "You know that's not what I meant. I just think you're going to be successful. You've already gotten a lot done, and it's only been a few months."

"Thanks," Flora said as the four of them trooped inside to clean their brushes. "It actually does mean a lot. Sometimes I still wonder if I'm in over my head."

"I don't think you are," Grady said. "I might have had my doubts when I first met you, but you've already learned a lot. I think you'll be able to make a living off of this if it's what you want to do."

"Won't you be kind of sad to leave, though?" Sydney asked. "After putting in so much work, I can't imagine wanting to walk away from it all."

Flora remained silent for a moment as she turned on the water in the kitchen sink and began washing the paintbrushes. As eager as she was to get the house in tip-top shape and to begin paying her aunt back for the loan that had enabled her to pull up her roots in Chicago and buy this place, she had been trying not to think about what would happen when the day came to actually sell it. Sydney was right—it would be bitter-sweet. She liked Warbler, and she liked the friends she had made.

"It *will* be sad," she admitted. "But it'll also be a little exciting. I'll have learned so much by then, and I'll actually know what I'm doing when I start over some-where new. And who knows, maybe I won't even have to move that far. I could buy another house somewhere in the area."

"Yeah, but you'd make more money if you bought and sold houses in a more desirable area, wouldn't you?" Violet pointed out. "I mean, I'm sure you'll be able to sell this one, no problem, but it's not like a ton of people want to move to Warbler. If you started flipping houses in, like, New York, you'd probably be able to make a larger profit."

Flora knew that was true. And realistically, it was probably what she would end up doing. Not in New York, but back in the Chicago area, where most of her family and her old friends all still lived. Still, it wasn't something she had to dwell on right now. She pushed the thought aside and finished rinsing out the brushes.

"We might have more people moving out of Warbler than into it soon," Sydney mused. "With this sort of violent crime on the rise, people might not feel safe here anymore. They still haven't caught whoever shot your neighbor, have they?"

"Not that I know of," Flora said with a sigh. "Unless someone comes forward with an eyewitness account of what happened or they uncover forensic evidence, I think they're going to be out of luck. They questioned everyone who lives on this road, but no one saw anything out of the ordinary."

"I don't believe no one knows what happened," Grady muttered. "Everyone in town knows everyone else's business."

"Maybe it was an accident," Violet suggested. "Someone could have been out target shooting and might not even be aware that a missed shot hit someone. It makes the most sense. It's not like we have gangs here. I didn't know the guy who died, but a few people who have come into my coffee shop did, and he sounded like a normal person."

Before Flora could answer with the confirmation that everything she knew about Spencer and everything Beth had said agreed that he was just a normal guy, her phone buzzed. She patted her hands dry on the dish towel and pulled her cell phone out of her back pocket to check it. The notification was from her front camera, which had sensed motion. A second later, someone knocked on the front door.

"I'll go get it, it's probably just my neighbor," she said.

Sure enough, Beth was at the front door. She had an eager look on her face. "I'm sorry if I'm disturbing a get together, but Natalie is home. Can you give me a ride over to her house so I can give her the casserole?"

"It's been a few days," Flora said. "Is the casserole even still good?"

"Tim and I ate the old one for dinner last night. I made a new one. It will only take a couple of minutes."

Flora looked over her shoulder to see her friends had followed her into the hall. "If you guys want to start the bonfire, go ahead. I'm going to run Beth next door really quickly."

She grabbed her purse, gave them a quick wave good-bye, and stepped out of the house. She didn't have any qualms about leaving her friends there. She trusted Violet and Grady completely and was beginning to trust Sydney too. They had all been through a lot together, and that sort of experience seemed to strengthen the bonds of friendship.

"Let's go," she said to Beth. She tried not to sound like it was a chore, because she knew how important this was to the older woman. "Is Tim coming along?"

"No, I'm going to ask him to stay at home," Beth said. "You know how his memory is. If he slips while we're visiting and mentions something about Spencer, it might upset Natalie."

Flora nodded and got into her truck. Beth got into the passenger seat, and she had to do some creative maneuvering to back out around the other vehicles, but soon they were out on the road. She stopped by Beth's house so the other woman could run inside and grab the casserole, then they continued down the road and around the curve to the Wolperts' house.

A dark red sedan was sitting in the driveway in front of the garage. Flora pulled up alongside it and got out of the truck, then reached across the seat to take the casserole from Beth so the older woman could climb down without having to balance it. She carried it up the steps to the front door and let Beth be the one who knocked. There was silence for a few moments, then Flora heard the sound of someone turning the deadbolt, and the door opened to reveal Natalie. Her brown hair hung around her face, and she had dark circles under her eyes.

"Hi," she mumbled, looking between Flora and Beth. "How can I help you?"

"I made a casserole for you, dear," Beth said. "You shouldn't have to worry about cooking at a time like this. Can we come in?"

Flora narrowed her eyes and looked over at Beth. She hoped the other woman wasn't going to try to get information out of Natalie. Now wasn't the time. She had expected that they would just hand the casserole over and leave.

Natalie sighed. "All right. You can bring it into the kitchen."

Flora stepped into the house uncertainly. It had a nice, homey feel. A pair of parakeets fluttered around in a cage in the corner, and there was a homemade Afghan spread out across the leather couch. The two of them followed Natalie through the house to the kitchen, which was filled with flower arrangements. Flora put the casserole down next to one of the vases, careful not to knock it over.

"How have you been holding up, dear? Do you want someone to come stay with you?" Beth asked. "It breaks my heart to think of you here all alone."

"Thanks for the offer, but I'd rather be here by myself," Natalie said quietly. "I've been staying with Cameron, my brother, but it got too suffocating. I just need some space, I'm sure you understand."

"Of course, dear," Beth said. "Whatever you need. You still have my phone number, don't you? You can call me at any time, even the middle of the night, and I'll come right over."

Natalie gave her a tight smile. "Thanks. And thank you for the casserole. I'm sure it's delicious; your food always is. If that's all…"

It was obvious to Flora they were being asked to leave, but Beth pulled out one of the stools by the counter and sat down on it.

"I hate to bring this up now, but it might be pertinent." She hesitated, and Flora began to feel creeping dread. Beth's eyes rose to meet Natalie's. "Were you aware your husband was having an affair with a woman named Kaylin Howard?"

CHAPTER FIVE

Flora's eyes widened in the same moment Natalie's expression shuttered. "You... How dare you?" she gasped. "You have no right!"

Beth didn't flinch. "I just wanted to make sure you knew about it, dear."

"My marriage is none of your business. I assure you, I was well aware of my husband's indiscretions, and it's something we were working on. It has nothing to do with what happened to him. Now, get out, both of you."

Beth eased off the stool. "Just as long as you knew, dear."

"Out," Natalie snapped, pointing toward the door.

"I'm sorry," Flora said, backing away. "I had no idea—"

"I don't care," she snarled. "Just get out!"

Flora and Beth hurried for the exit. Flora was shaking as she climbed into her truck. As soon as Beth closed the passenger side door, she rounded on the older woman.

"How could you do that?" she whispered. "Beth, that was terrible. Her husband just *died*. She didn't need that."

"Can't you see how it's important?" Beth asked. "If she didn't know, then she wouldn't have told the police about it. That young man was murdered in cold blood, in his own front yard. Something like an affair could very well be the reason behind it."

"Then it's something *you* should've told the police," Flora said as she turned the truck on and slammed it into reverse. "You don't go up to a grieving widow and tell her about her husband's infidelity."

"She already knew, so it's not as if I've done any harm," Beth muttered, crossing her arms.

Flora glared at her but kept her jaw clenched shut. Arguing was useless, and the damage was already done. She kept up a fuming silence as she drove back to Beth's house and pulled into the driveway to let the older woman out. Once she was out of the truck, Beth opened her mouth as if she was going to say something else, but Flora leaned over and slammed the passenger door shut. She backed out of the driveway, leaving Beth standing there, clearly upset.

Flora pulled into her own driveway and got out of her truck, taking a deep breath. She thought it would be best if she didn't talk to Beth for a while. She couldn't believe the older woman had done that; not only had she broached a sensitive topic to a woman who had just lost her husband, but she had made Flora an accomplice.

Her friends had gotten the fire started in the backyard, so after dropping her purse off in the house, Flora went through the back door to join them. They had pulled the camp chairs out from the shed, leaving one open for Flora next to Grady, and had brought out the drinks Flora had bought for the evening as well.

"Good, you're back," Violet said cheerfully. "How is —wait, why do you look so upset?"

41

"Beth," Flora ground out as she sat in her chair. Grady looked over at her, raising his eyebrows. She sighed. "Sometimes I think she's tolerable, but then she goes and does something like this."

Violet frowned. "You can't just leave it at that. What happened?"

Flora hesitated. "I'll tell you, but I don't want it spreading around town." She didn't think Grady would say anything, but she didn't know Sydney well enough to be certain, and Violet was a very social woman who owned a coffee shop. She wasn't as bad about gossip as Beth was, but she did like to talk.

"My lips are sealed," Violet promised.

Sydney made a zipping motion across his lips. "I won't say anything either."

Grady just nodded.

Flora exhaled. "Fine. Apparently, Beth knew Spencer Wolpert was having an affair. She thought that tonight, while we were dropping off the casserole, was the ideal time to tell his widow about it."

Grady's eyes widened, but it was Violet's gasp that was the most gratifying. "She did not. That's horrible!

How did your neighbor take it?"

"Natalie was livid, but she admitted she had known about the affair."

"Who was he having the affair with?" Violet asked.

Flora hesitated, but she'd already come this far. "Someone named Kaylin Howard? I don't know her."

Grady shrugged when she looked at him, but Sydney perked up. "I know her. She has a dog, one of those big white ones—a Great Pyrenees? She brings it into the feed store every other week when she stops in to buy dog food and chicken feed."

"I know her, too," Violet said. "She's a regular at the coffee shop. You might have bumped into her there at some point. She has blonde hair and always dresses nicely. I think she works at a dentist's office."

The description didn't ring a bell, but a new possibility occurred to her. "What kind of car does she drive?"

Violet gave her a blank look and a shrug, but Sydney said, "It's a silver sedan. I should know, I've helped her load the bags of feed into the trunk often enough. That big dog of hers takes up the whole backseat."

It made sense now, why Beth had pursed her lips at that silver car they had seen in the Wolperts' driveway. Kaylin had been parked outside of their house the evening after the murder. Had she been planning to meet with Spencer, or had she heard what happened and was there for another reason?

"You've seen her car?" Grady asked.

Flora nodded and told them about the first night she and Beth went over to try to deliver a casserole. "I don't know what it means, or if it means anything, but I think I should tell Officer Hendricks about it."

"Do you think Kaylin might have murdered him?" Violet asked, her eyes wide. "She comes in every morning during the week. I'm going to see her on Monday. How am I going to act normal while I'm serving her coffee?"

"I don't know," Sydney said. "She seems too normal to me."

"Don't they say the same thing about serial killers?" Grady asked. "Their neighbors always thought they were perfectly normal, quiet people."

"I've never met the woman, but looking at it from an outside perspective, it makes sense, doesn't it?" Flora mused. "Natalie said she was aware of her husband's affair, and they had been working on their relationship. That might mean Spencer tried to break things off with Kaylin. Maybe she got upset about it and decided to get revenge."

"But someone should have seen her car if she drove by and shot him. You don't get a lot of traffic on this road."

"We don't, but that doesn't mean we memorize every single car that goes by," Flora said. "The gunshot went off a few minutes after you left. I think there might have been one other car that went by, but I have no idea what type of vehicle it was. Other than the garbage truck, I don't remember there being any other traffic that afternoon." She glanced to Grady. "Do you?"

"No," he said. "I think you're right, there was a vehicle that went by right before Violet left, but I don't remember what kind either. That doesn't mean anything, though—whoever shot your neighbor could have come from the other direction."

"I wonder if the garbage truck driver saw anything," Flora mused. "He would have been parked in the road, and any vehicle that wanted to get by him would've had to slow down and go around. Maybe I can mention that to Officer Hendricks too. He could ask Cameron—" she broke off. "Hold on, Natalie said she was staying with her brother, Cameron. The guy who drives the garbage truck that picks up the garbage on my road is named Cameron. Do you think he's her brother?"

She looked to Grady, who frowned. "His last name is Banks, but I don't know if he has a sister."

"I don't know what Natalie's maiden name was," Flora said. "It might not even matter, I guess it's the sort of connection I should get used to now that I live in a small town."

"You should go talk to the police on Monday," Violet said. "I'm sure you'll feel better once you know they have all the information you do. There really isn't anything else you can do until then."

Flora sighed. "I know. I guess I'll spend tomorrow painting and trying to avoid Beth. I still can't believe she did that. She might have meant well, but it's a terrible thing to say to someone who just lost their spouse."

CHAPTER SIX

Flora kept to herself on Sunday, too ashamed to go try to talk to Natalie, though she did want to apologize more thoroughly at some point in the future. She was careful not to catch Beth's eye whenever the older woman went by her house on one of her walks, and Beth must have guessed she was still upset, because she didn't seek her out to chat like she usually would. She didn't like this new tension with her neighbor, but she also didn't want to forgive Beth just yet. As far as she was concerned, what the other woman had done was unimaginably cruel. What if Natalie hadn't known about the affair? Telling her about it wouldn't have done anything except cause further emotional trauma to a woman who had already lost everything.

Bright and early Monday morning, she went into town. She stopped by the police station, wondering what it said about her that she was becoming a regular there, and asked to see Officer Hendricks. She only had to wait a few minutes before he appeared and ushered her back to his office. She wasn't even sure if he was the lead investigator on the case, but she already had a rapport with him since he was always the one she talked to when something happened.

"How many skeletons have you found on your property this weekend?" he asked as he sat down at his desk. "Five? Ten? Have you uncovered a mass grave or an ancient temple?"

She rolled her eyes and sat in the chair opposite his desk. "Very funny. No, I haven't uncovered anything except for an affair."

He raised his eyebrows. "While I don't approve of anyone who is unfaithful in a monogamous relationship, it's not exactly something that falls under police purview."

"I think this one might," she said. "I learned, well, my neighbor Beth told me, but I also got confirmation from Natalie herself, that Spencer Wolpert was having an affair with a woman named Kaylin Howard."

Officer Hendricks frowned, which made her guess this was news to him. "I see. We'll have to get Ms. Wolpert to confirm this, of course, but it might be the break in the case we need. Do you have any other information that might be helpful?"

"This is more of a guess, but the night of the murder, Beth York and I went over to the Wolperts' house because Beth wanted to see if Natalie was home so she could deliver a homemade casserole to her. When we got there, someone was sitting in a silver car in the driveway. They left as soon as I put my blinker on to turn in. And according to a friend of mine, Kaylin Howard drives a silver car. I don't know for sure it was her because I didn't see her face, and I have no idea why she would be there, but after learning about the affair, I realized it might be important information."

He made a note on the notepad in front of him. "I see. Thank you for bringing this to my attention, Ms. Abner. Is there anything you'd like to tell me?"

Flora shook her head. "That's all I can think of. Have you made any progress on the case?"

"Officially? No. Unofficially? I'm not supposed to say anything, but also no. Hopefully, this gives us what we need to find some leads."

He thanked her again and escorted her to the exit. She waved goodbye as she got back into her truck. As she started it, she wondered why neither Beth nor Natalie had mentioned the affair to him. She could understand why Natalie had kept it quiet, but Beth loved to talk. What reason did the older woman have to hide the affair from the police?

She didn't have any other errands to run in town that morning, but she *could* use a pick-me-up. She decided to swing by Violet Delights and kill two birds with one stone by getting a delicious latte and saying hi to her friend at the same time. Traffic in Warbler never got really bad like it did in Chicago, but she had managed to hit the morning rush hour, so she had to park a little farther down the block than usual when she got to the coffee shop.

She enjoyed the mild morning weather as she walked down the sidewalk, glancing in through the windows of the various shops as she went. She liked living in Warbler more than she had expected and tried not to think about how much she would miss it when it was time to leave.

When she reached Violet Delights, she pushed the door open and stepped inside. The scents of coffee, caramel, and something fruity wrapped around her as she walked into the vividly purple business. *Everything* was done up in shades of purple, including the tables and chairs. Violet was talking with a customer, but she looked up and gave Flora a wink as she came in. The purple contacts she wore always made her gaze a little unsettling, and Flora wondered, not for the first time, if the other woman's obsession with the color purple had stemmed from her name, or if she would have loved the color even if she had been named something else.

She waited in line for her turn, and when she got to the counter, she ordered her usual: a white chocolate caramel latte. Violet started making it, familiar enough with all of the drinks she served that she could focus most of her attention on chatting with Flora.

"I don't usually see you in town this early," she said. "How has your morning been so far?"

"Good." Flora paused to glance around, but no one was standing particularly close to her. She lowered her voice. "I stopped by the police station already."

"Good," Violet said with a firm nod. "Do you feel better now?"

"I do. It's good to know that whatever happens, it's all out of my hands now."

Violet put the finishing touches on the coffee, but instead of handing it over, she leaned forward. Flora mirrored her, and Violet whispered, "Guess who stopped in this morning?" Instead of waiting for Flora to guess, she plowed ahead. "Kaylin Howard. And she was a wreck. It looked like she spent all weekend crying. I wasn't sure whether to feel bad for her, or if I should just try to get her out of here as quickly as possible."

"If she *is* guilty, the police will be on her trail now," Flora whispered back as she accepted the latte. "I'll let you know if I hear anything."

"Thanks," Violet said as she straightened up. "Have a good day. I'll see you later."

Flora nodded to her friend as Violet turned her attention to her next customer. She wished she knew what it meant that Kaylin had been upset. Was it a normal reaction to the death of someone she cared about, or was there more to it?

CHAPTER SEVEN

Flora sipped her latte as she drove home. And the old house really had become *home* to her, though it had a very different feel from her apartment back in Chicago. The apartment had been a sanctuary, the perfect place to escape from her hectic life and both figuratively and literally be above it all. She missed some things about it, such as the wonderful view of Chicago from her windows, the endless hot water, and the perfect climate control. She missed being able to order food from any restaurant imaginable and have it delivered to her door in twenty minutes. She missed being able to walk anywhere she wanted, and even missed the weekly Friday night dinners with her family, though in practice they had frequently been a source of irritation to her.

The house was a different sort of sanctuary entirely. It wasn't the place she went to escape, because most of the time, she had nothing she wanted to escape from. She didn't need to desperately seize the moments of quiet in between her busy work and social activities. The house wasn't a refuge as much as her apartment had been. It was simply her place. It was a building she was growing to know like the back of her hand, imperfections and all. It was her hope for the future, and the location of a lot of happy evenings with her friends.

When she got back, she spent a little time inside, petting her cat while she finished her coffee and watched the news. Once her latte was gone, she changed into clothes she wouldn't mind getting paint on and went outside to start painting the back of her house. A glance at the lawn told her it would be time to mow again soon, but that would have to wait until tomorrow, after the paint had time to dry. The last thing she needed was to send dust and bits of freshly cut grass swirling into the air to get caught up in the wet paint on the house's siding.

She had chosen to work on the back of the house since it would keep her out of view of the road, but her desire to continue avoiding Beth was in vain.

"There you are."

Flora, who had been halfway up the ladder with a paintbrush in her hand, yelped and almost dropped it in an attempt to steady herself. She glowered down at the older woman, who was standing in her yard, looking up at her with one hand on her hip and the other holding onto her basset hound's leash. Grumbling to herself, Flora made her way down the ladder and took her phone out of her pocket to pause the music that was playing.

"What do you want?"

"Don't be rude," Beth snipped. "I know you're upset with me, but you can't avoid me forever. Aren't we friends, Flora? I've only ever been kind to you."

Flora sighed and dropped her paintbrush next to the can of paint. "Look, I think what you did to Natalie was cruel. What I'm really upset about, though, is the fact that you involved me in it without talking to me first. That wasn't fair, Beth. It made me feel like you manipulated me."

The older woman's face creased into a frown. "I didn't mean it like that, dear. I hope you believe me when I say I truly wasn't planning on asking about the affair when I asked you to drive me over. It just popped out."

"I don't know if I believe that," Flora admitted, crossing her arms. "And I still don't think you should have brought it up. If you knew about the affair, why wouldn't you have said something when Spencer was still alive?"

"I did," Beth said. "I talked to Spencer about it. He asked me to give him time to talk to Natalie himself. That was just a few weeks ago. I figured I would give the boy a month and see what happened. I was keeping my eye out to see if that horrible woman came back again. If she had, I would have taken matters into my own hands. I'm still not sure if they really stopped seeing each other, or if that horrible woman just started avoiding my house and came to see him from the other direction down the road."

"How did you know about the affair?" Flora asked, curious despite herself.

"You know how many walks Sammy and I take," Beth said, stooping to pat the dog's head. "I saw that silver car parked in his driveway frequently. Poor Natalie works in an office, but Spencer worked at home. I admit I was curious about who was visiting him so much. I made it a point to keep an eye on the situation, and one day I saw that woman kiss him goodbye when she was leaving. That was when I confronted him. I can't *stand* people who cheat on their partners, but I thought I would give him the benefit of the doubt and let him come clean on his own. Now, I regret that. I only hope what happened to him has nothing to do with the affair. I..." Here, Beth paused, casting her eyes downward. "I was overcome with guilt when I realized I might have been able to prevent what happened if only I had told Natalie the truth directly. I'm sorry for involving you, Flora. I didn't mean to put you in such an awkward position."

Flora sighed. Already, her anger at the older woman was fading. Beth might be a meddler, but she did have a good heart. "All right. Just ... don't do it again, okay?"

"I'll do my best never to put you in that position again."

Flora nodded. That would have to be good enough for her. "Out of curiosity," she mused, letting her arms uncross. "Do you happen to know Natalie's maiden name?"

Beth gave a considering frown. "I believe it's Banks. I know her family is from the area. Why do you ask?"

"She mentioned that her brother's name is Cameron, so it made me wonder if she was related to our garbage truck driver."

"Oh, yes. You could've just asked me. He's her brother. I make sure to bring a little treat out for him whenever I see him pull up for the garbage."

"I see." She made a mental note to give Cameron her condolences about his brother-in-law the next time she saw him. He wasn't her friend, exactly, but he was an acquaintance, and he was friends with Grady. Sometimes it still boggled her mind just how connected everything was in Warbler.

"Would you like to chat more, dear?" Beth said. "I could sure go for a glass of that lemonade you make. Or if you would like to come over to my house, I could make us some tea. I'm sure Tim would love to see you."

Flora hesitated, glancing at her house. She was only a third of the way done with painting the back, but it was still pretty early in the day, and she could afford a break.

"If you don't mind me coming over in my painting clothes, that sounds lovely."

Beth gave her a smile filled with genuine warmth. Flora returned it, glad she had patched things up with her neighbor.

CHAPTER EIGHT

It wasn't until Wednesday that she and Grady, who had taken advantage of a day off to come and help her, finished painting her house's siding. It was a big achievement, and the house looked much better. Sure, the porch was still sagging and some of the windows didn't match the others, and the overgrown driveway and empty flowerbeds out front weren't doing her any favors, but overall, the house was actually pleasant to look at now.

She wiped at her sweaty forehead, wincing when the paint on her fingers smeared across her forehead. "It's finally done," she breathed. "Thanks so much, Grady. I really appreciate your help." She had long since stopped offering to pay him. They had moved from acquaintances of convenience to having a solid friendship, and she thought offering him money now would just offend him. Still... "If there's anything you ever need help with, just let me know."

He grunted, neither accepting nor declining. "We did a good job. What are you going to work on next?"

"Well, I did want to get that entrance hallway painted, but if I'm being honest, I'm kind of tired of painting. I think I might do some gardening. A few flowers would make this place look even better. After that, I'll go through my list and find the next big project to focus on."

"I know someone who can get you gravel for the driveway," he offered, eyeing it. It really was an eyesore and was horribly bumpy. She winced whenever she drove over the biggest pothole, even if the truck was moving at a crawl.

"Leave me their number, I'll probably still do some shopping around for prices, but I'll call them first. For now, let's get cleaned up. I am so ready to not be covered in paint."

They moved to the relatively cool interior of the house. Amaretto rubbed against her leg, hoping for a pet, but Flora didn't want to get any paint on her fur. She made kissing noises at the cat instead, and gently nudged her out of the way so she could shut the door. After that, she went upstairs to take a quick shower and get changed. Feeling refreshed, she returned downstairs to find Grady, who had washed up in the kitchen sink, trapped on the couch with Amaretto in his lap. The cat was kneading his jeans with her claws, and Flora grinned.

"See? I told you she would warm up to you. Good luck getting her to leave you alone now. Do you want some lemonade?"

He gave her an affirmative answer, so she fetched glasses for them both and then joined him on the couch.

"I know it's still early, but I don't think I'm going to do anything else today. I'm just going to sit back, relax, and enjoy the satisfaction that comes from finishing a project."

"If you don't need to get anything else done, do you want me to head out?"

She shook her head. "No way. You're welcome to stay and keep me company, unless there's something else you need to do." In truth, she no longer felt quite as comfortable alone at her house as she used to, not with the mystery of who killed Spencer Wolpert still ongoing.

Her face must have betrayed her thoughts, because Grady said, "Still no word on who shot your neighbor?"

She sighed. "Not that I've heard. It's not as if I'm directly connected to the case, so the police aren't giving me any updates. And I'm definitely not about to go ask Natalie about it." The poor woman didn't need anyone else dredging up bad thoughts for her.

"Want me to ask Cameron?" he suggested. "I see him around town sometimes. He might know what's going on."

She bit her lip, considering the offer. "That's a good idea. I don't need you to ask for me, though. I'll keep an eye out for the garbage truck when it comes tomorrow, and I'll ask him then. Unless you think he wouldn't be willing to talk to me."

"I think he will," he said. "He'll understand why you're concerned."

She was considering the best way to approach the man with her question when someone knocked on her door. She had left her phone face down on the coffee table, so she didn't get the benefit of the security camera's early warning. Sighing, she stood up. "It's probably Beth. I'm glad we're on speaking terms again, but I'll tell her I'm busy right now. Well, after I make her admire my house."

Grinning, and eager to show off what she had accomplished, she got up to answer the door. She faltered when, through the glass pane in the door, she saw not Beth's familiar face, but Natalie's. She hadn't thought to expect a visit from the other woman, and her mind was blank as she pulled the door open.

"Sorry to bother you," Natalie said, looking awkward. "But could I ask you for a favor?"

"Of course," Flora said. "Do you want to come in?" The other woman shook her head, so Flora stepped outside instead, pulling the door shut behind her. "My cat likes to try sneaking out whenever the door is open," she explained. "Before you say whatever's on your mind, I just want to apologize again. I had no idea that Beth was going to say what she said, and I feel horrible about it."

Natalie's eyes widened slightly. "Oh. Thank you for saying that, but I feel like I should be the one to apologize. I lost my temper. I guess it's understandable why I did, but I still feel bad about snapping at you."

Flora smiled and held out her hand to shake. "Well, I'm happy to let bygones be bygones if you are."

Natalie shook her hand. "Good. I'm glad that's out of the way. What I came to ask you was sort of related to it. You're friends with Beth, right?"

"Yeah," Flora admitted. Somehow, Beth had wormed her way past acquaintance to friend as well. "We've gotten pretty close. Did you need to talk to her? I'm sure she wouldn't mind if you called her."

"No, that's actually the opposite of what I want," Natalie said. "I was hoping you could get her to leave me alone."

Flora frowned. "Has she been bothering you?"

"She's been coming over every single day, trying to get me to talk to her," Natalie said, crossing her arms. "I've told her repeatedly that I don't want to talk and that I just want to be left alone, but she's not listening to me. I was hoping you could say something to her."

"I'll try," Flora said. "If I'm being honest, I'm not sure how well she'll listen to me. She seems pretty stubborn."

"I know she is, and it's driving me crazy," Natalie said. "I don't know how she knew about ... about Spencer, but I don't want to talk about it. Not with her, not with anyone. I just want everyone to leave me be and let me grieve how I want to grieve. I'm getting sick and tired of her pestering me every single day."

The other woman's voice grew more and more vehement as she went on. Flora winced. "All right. I'll talk to her," she promised. "I'll do my best to convince her to give it a rest."

"Thank you," Natalie said. "I'm sure I'll see you around. If you manage to get her to leave me be, I'll owe you one." With that, Natalie returned to her car, which was parked next to Grady's truck in the driveway. Flora watched her get into the vehicle, then stepped back into the house. She wasn't looking forward to the conversation she needed to have with Beth. She couldn't envision it going well. Beth seemed like the sort of person who was too used to getting what she wanted to give up without a fight.

CHAPTER NINE

Flora didn't want to miss Cameron when he came to pick up the garbage the next day, but he always came around the same time in the afternoon, so she took advantage of the morning to go buy some flowers from the local nursery. She chose some brightly colored white and red ones and grabbed a few bags of mulch while she was at it. She had never been very into gardening, but just like everything else, it was something she could learn. She had the forethought to buy a trowel as well and returned to her home armed with all the tools she needed to continue beautifying her yard. She knew the flowers didn't really matter, not for flipping the house — these would be long dead by the time it came to sell it—but she liked the thought of making her property look good.

After dragging the dumpster to the road, she changed into jeans and an old T-shirt, tied her hair back, and got to work.

She had finished weeding and planting one of the flowerbeds and was in the middle of spreading mulch around—she used her fingers but wished she had bought a small rake—when she heard the familiar sound of the garbage truck pulling up the road. She brushed her hands off and rose to her feet, walking down to the dumpster to greet Cameron. The garbage truck stopped with a hiss of air brakes, and Cameron jumped out with his usual good cheer.

"Hey," he said, looking around her property. "No Grady today?"

"He's at work," she said. "Just me today, I'm afraid."

"Hey, I'm always glad to see a friendly face. Your house is looking good. The two of you have made a lot of progress on it."

He always seemed to speak of them as a pair when she talked to him, and she wondered if he thought they were dating. It didn't matter—that wasn't what she wanted to talk to him about. "Can I get you some lemonade?" she offered.

"Not today, I'm afraid," he said. "I'm hoping to catch my sister before she leaves. I think she's off work for another week, but she mentioned something about having an appointment this afternoon."

That gave her the perfect opportunity to ask what she wanted to ask. "Oh, so you and Natalie are related? She mentioned your name, but I wasn't certain."

"Yeah. She's my little sister." He dragged the dumpster around to the back of the truck, and she followed. "I'm sure you heard what happened to her good-for-nothing husband. She's been taking it hard, and I wanted to see how she's doing. She was staying with me at first, but I think I was being a little overbearing."

"I take it you didn't like Spencer, then?" she asked, pretending idle curiosity.

"I couldn't stand the man," Cameron admitted. He paused while the dump truck's mechanical arm emptied the garbage bin, then said, "I'm not sure she'd like it if I said why."

"I heard about the affair," she admitted. "I'm really sorry she had to go through that, and then his death on top of it. I don't know her well, but I feel terrible for her."

"He had it coming, if you ask me. I hope she gets over it soon and finds someone better to share her life with."

"Do you know if the police have made any progress on the case?" Flora asked, taking the dumpster from him to drag it back onto her property. "I've been keeping my eyes and ears peeled for any news, but I haven't heard a thing. It's scary to think that there's someone out there who killed someone, and no one knows who it is. It makes me wonder if I'm safe, living here on my own."

"No, I don't think the police have made any progress," he said, scratching at the back of his head. "I don't think you have to worry, though. I doubt it was just random violence. That sort of thing doesn't really happen in Warbler."

"I'll try to keep that in mind," she said. She waved as he hopped back into his truck. "See you around, Cameron."

She watched as he drove off, then returned to the flowerbeds, kneeling down to finish her work. As she spread the mulch out and then moved over to the second flower bed to begin pulling the weeds out, she pondered over the conversation. From the sound of it, Cameron certainly wasn't broken up about his brother-in-law's death at all. She could understand that if Natalie had told him about the affair. *She* certainly wouldn't harbor any tender feelings toward either of her siblings' spouses if she found out they had been having an affair. Still, she couldn't help but wonder if he knew more than he was saying about the murder. She would have expected him to be more concerned about his sister's safety, but he hadn't brought it up once.

She had just started planting the second set of flowers when her cell phone began to ring. She wiped her hands off on her jeans and pulled it out of her back pocket, only to blink at the sight of her aunt's name on the screen. Sliding her thumb across the screen, she answered the call.

"Hi, Aunt Olivia," she said, turning so she was seated on one of the stones that bordered the flowerbeds.

"Hi, Flora," her aunt said. "How are you doing? Your parents told me they haven't visited yet, so I decided to check up on you. How is the house coming along? Are you happy?"

"The house is coming along great," she said, glancing up at it. "I'll send you some pictures, if you want. And no, I still haven't had anyone out to see it. I'll have to invite Mom and Dad later. I want to get more of the interior complete before they visit."

"But you're still content with your choices?" her aunt asked.

Flora nodded, even though the older woman couldn't see it. "I am. I know I've said it already, but thank you so much, Aunt Olivia. I'm happy here. I feel like I can breathe again. And I love what I've been doing, even if it's hard sometimes. How are *you*?"

"Oh, my life is the same as always," her aunt replied. "I'm just glad you're happy. Now, I'm going to be visiting your parents for Christmas, but what would you think of me coming your way for Thanksgiving?"

Thanksgiving was still months off. Flora was certain she could have one of the extra rooms done up as a nice guest room by then. "That would be great. Just let me know how long you think you'll be staying, and I'll have everything ready."

She and her aunt said their goodbyes, and she ended the call. She had never hosted a holiday on her own before. Should she invite the rest of her family too? She wasn't sure if they would come—they had their own traditions, and Kentucky was a long way to travel from Illinois, but she could decide that later. For now, she got back to work on the flowerbeds.

The brief talk with her aunt had pushed thoughts of the murder to the back of her mind. It had been a good reminder of why she was here and what the bigger picture was. It didn't feel right to call her neighbor's death small-town drama, but getting involved in it certainly was. She wasn't a police officer or a private investigator. She was just Flora, a woman who wanted to flip houses for a living and wasn't afraid of getting her hands dirty. She had her own life to focus on.

She would have to leave solving murders to the professionals.

CHAPTER TEN

Grady came over later that evening to help her decide what her next big project should be. She had a few promising options written out on a list on her phone, but Grady had his own ideas. He led her around to the back of the house and scowled at the shed.

"You still didn't catch it?"

She shook her head. "Nothing since that opossum."

For over a month now, she had been having problems with a raccoon that had set up residence in her shed. She had bought a live trap in an attempt to capture it, but the beast seemed unusually smart. The only thing she had managed to catch was a single, young opossum, which Grady had convinced her to simply release on her property, stating that they were good animals to have around. She hadn't seen it again, so at least it was making less of a pest of itself than the raccoon was. The raccoon made itself known almost every morning when she woke up and checked the footage her security cameras had captured during the night. It liked to sniff around her house before retreating into the shed for the day, and she suspected it was living somewhere in the loft above the main part of the shed. The wood was decayed enough that Grady didn't think it was safe to go up and try to chase it out.

She wouldn't mind so much if it wasn't for the fact that it had gotten into her dumpster twice and made a mess of things. That, and what it left behind. Finding raccoon leavings on her lawnmower had been the last straw for her.

"We need to get this fixed up," he declared, frowning at the ramshackle building.

"I thought you said it was safe," she said, turning to him in horror. "I've been storing stuff in there. Are you telling me it's about to collapse on my head?"

"I said it's safe for now," he corrected her. "It's just going to keep getting worse, though. Give it a year, and it might collapse."

She wilted. "All right, how hard is it going to be to fix?"

"We're going to have to shore up some of the supports. You're going to need some four-by-fours and the means to attach them, along with some cement. You'll also want to redo the roof and fix the rafters and the plywood in the loft. Some of the siding needs to be replaced too. While you're at it, you might as well drag everything out, grade the floor, and lay down some wood."

"That … sounds like a big project."

He raised an eyebrow, amused. "I thought you weren't afraid of big projects."

She wrinkled her nose. "It's one thing when it comes to the house, but the shed? That feels like a waste of time. No one is going to buy the house just for the shed. Do you think it would be easier just to knock it down?"

"Not necessarily," he said. "Besides, where would you store your things? You would need to build or buy a replacement, which would be a lot more diffi-cult, not to mention more expensive than just fixing this one. That's not even getting started on the permits."

"Fine, you win," she groaned. "We'll fix the shed."

"On the plus side, I bet we'll chase the raccoon away, and we will be able to make sure the shed is solid enough that it can't get back in."

She perked up a little. "All right. Let's go in and make a list. I'll start buying things this weekend."

She would start tomorrow, but she still wanted to get that entrance hallway painted. She had taken all the wallpaper off of the walls a while ago and had put off painting it for nearly a month now.

Grady nodded, and they started walking around the side of the house. As the road came into view, Flora spotted Beth and Sammy returning from one of their walks.

"Hold on just a second," she said to Grady. "I still need to talk to Beth about leaving Natalie be."

She jogged toward the road, calling out to Beth, who turned to her with a wave. Sammy strained forward on his leash to sniff her shoes, and she bent down to scratch the dog behind his droopy ears before straightening up. "Hey, I've been looking for you. Do you have a minute to talk?"

"I do," Beth said, moving over to the side of the road. "Is everything all right, dear?"

"Yeah, I just wanted to ask…" This was a little more awkward than she had anticipated. She pulled her fingers through her ponytail, wincing at one of the tangles. "Well, the thing is, Natalie stopped by my house yesterday—"

"Oh, that's wonderful. How is she doing? I've barely been able to speak to her since the incident."

"That's the thing," Flora said. "She asked me to ask you to give her some space."

Beth's face fell. "Oh. I see."

"I think she's just feeling crowded right now," Flora hurried to explain. "She doesn't want to talk to anyone, it's not just you."

"It can't be good for her to be shut up in that house all alone," Beth said. "I think she needs to talk to people, if she ever wants to get past what happened."

"It's only been a week," Flora said. "You should give her more time, Beth. Can you please stop going over there for a couple of weeks, at least? You should respect what she wants."

Beth frowned. "Well, I suppose I can give her some time to figure things out on her own. I just hope she knows she can come to me if she needs anything."

"She does," Flora promised. "Thanks, Beth."

"I know you're only trying to help her, dear," Beth said, reaching out to pat her arm. "You're a kind girl. Now that I have you, I've been meaning to ask you something as well."

"What is it?" Flora asked, relaxing now that the difficult part of the conversation was over.

"Has your garbage pickup been late recently? A few of my friends from farther down the road have been complaining about it. I don't always pay attention to when the garbage comes, so I haven't noticed anything."

"No, Cameron still comes at the same time as always," Flora said. "If it was late this morning, it's probably because he was caught up in talking to his sister. She's not working right now, and I know he wanted to spend some time checking in on her."

"I don't think it's that," Beth said. "He was late last week too. I'll just have to tell them that you haven't noticed anything either. They don't want to call in to complain over such a little matter, but they do like knowing their garbage will be picked up by a certain time."

Flora didn't think she would notice if the garbage pickup came late or not, unless she was specifically waiting for Cameron, but she just smiled and nodded. "Well, I'd better get going. I have company."

She saw the older woman's eyes flick over to her driveway. "I saw. That Grady Barnes again? The two of you sure are close."

"He's been a big help with the house," Flora told her.

"I'm sure he has," Beth said. "Just keep in mind, a nice girl like you has lots of options. Why, my nephew—"

"I really need to get going, Beth," Flora said, backing away from her. The last thing she needed was for the older woman to try to set her up on some sort of blind date. "Have a nice evening."

She hurried away before the older woman could draw her back into conversation. All that really mattered was that she had passed along Natalie's message. She couldn't do more than that. She just hoped the older woman would stick to her word and quit bothering Natalie.

She was glad to get back to Grady. They went inside the house and, after she fed her cat dinner, they sat at the kitchen table with two glasses of lemonade while Grady helped her make the list of the things she needed to fix up the shed.

Despite her reluctance to spend time on the shed, she had to admit it was a little exciting to be starting a new project. And it would be nice to have the shed in good condition. Getting rid of the raccoon was just a bonus.

CHAPTER ELEVEN

Saturday afternoon found Flora sitting on her porch in one of the rocking chairs she had bought two weeks ago. She had a glass of lemonade in one hand and was scrolling through her phone's social media feed in the other. She felt pleasantly tired, her muscles loose from all of the heavy lifting she had done. She'd spent the earlier part of the day getting everything she would need to fix the shed from the hardware store. Grady had offered to come over later to help her unload it, but she had told him she could handle it, and handle it she did. She had backed her truck up to the shed and had dragged the heavy four-by-fours out of the bed of the truck and into the shelter of the shed. They were safely under the shed's roof now, covered by a tarp to protect them from the irritating raccoon. The only things she hadn't gotten were the sheets of metal for the roof. Grady was insistent that they could do it themselves, but the hardware store was going to have to special order them for her.

All in all, she felt good. The house was looking better than ever, and it had sent a surge of joy through her to see the new, white paint on the siding and the pretty flowers in the flowerbeds by the front porch when she pulled up with the supplies. Soon, she would get the driveway redone as well. She wanted to find some crushed white stone for it, to match the white siding and the white of the flowers she had chosen.

She was planning on spending the afternoon mowing after her short break. After that, she thought she would order a pizza and spend the evening relaxing with Amaretto. She also wanted to call her parents and check in with them. She was missing her family more and more as time went on, and she knew she would have to schedule a visit soon. She wondered if it would feel strange to return to Chicago after the more slow-paced, peaceful life here in Warbler. It had only been a few months, but she felt like a completely different person.

She put her phone down and leaned her head back against the chair, enjoying the calm feel of the day. It wasn't until she heard the sound of a car approaching that she looked up, sipping her lemonade as she watched the vehicle approach. She didn't think she would ever be as bad as Beth was when it came to looking for sources of gossip, but she could admit that she enjoyed watching the world go by. Everything in Warbler was so connected, and she wanted to be a part of that connection, even though she was planning on leaving in just under two years.

Her gaze sharpened when she realized the vehicle that was approaching was a silver sedan. She was almost certain it was the same one she and Beth had seen sitting in the Wolperts' driveway the evening of the murder. She squinted as it went by. There was no big, white dog in the back seat, but the woman behind the steering wheel was blonde, which matched Violet's description of Kaylin Howard. The woman didn't glance at her as she drove past Flora's house. Flora watched the car as it continued down the road, eventually disappearing around the curve past Beth's place.

Was Kaylin going to the Wolperts' house? Was she expecting Natalie to be at work? The question of why burned inside of her. What could she possibly hope to gain from going to the house where her now deceased affair partner lived?

I wish I had Natalie's number, she thought, looking down at her phone. It hadn't occurred to her to get it from the other woman, but now, she wished she could give her a heads-up that Kaylin might be heading her way. If Natalie didn't appreciate Beth trying to get her to talk, she doubted Natalie would appreciate Kaylin appearing in her driveway.

Frowning, she picked her phone up and scrolled through her contacts list until she found Beth's number. She called, but it rang through to voicemail. Neither Beth nor Tim drove, but there was a service that came and picked them up a couple times a week so they could go into town for shopping and appointments. She tried to remember if the bus had come for them that day. She didn't remember it, but since she had been gone all morning, she could easily have missed it. It was a Saturday, though, and she knew Beth liked going shopping on the weekends.

She tapped her fingers on the wooden armrest of the rocking chair, considering her options. It wasn't her job to get involved in this, but she knew how desperately Natalie just wanted to be left alone. Maybe she should drive by the other woman's house and see if Kaylin was there. Natalie might appreciate a third party on the scene if there did end up being some sort of confrontation.

The knowledge that Kaylin was, as far as she was aware, the only real suspect in the case was what eventually pushed her over the edge to action. She had no idea what Kaylin was doing here, or if the person who was behind the wheel of that silver sedan even *was* Kaylin, but she couldn't, in good conscience, let Natalie come face to face alone with the woman who might have murdered her husband when she could do something about it.

She drained the rest of her lemonade, then ducked back inside to put the glass in the kitchen and grab her purse. After locking the door behind her, she got into her truck and pulled out of the driveway, wincing as the vehicle bumped over the big pothole. She eased her way around the curve in the road, hoping she had been wrong, and that Natalie's dark red sedan would be the only vehicle in her driveway.

Unfortunately, her gut feeling had been right. Natalie's sedan was there, and the silver car was parked behind it. There was also a third vehicle she didn't recognize, a black SUV.

As she slowed, she spotted two women standing on the porch. One was Natalie, her arms crossed over her chest and her posture defensive. The other was the blonde woman, who was gesticulating wildly with her hands. It definitely looked like Natalie could use some help. Flora pulled into the driveway, causing both women to look around. She hesitated for a second, but Natalie was looking right at her and wasn't gesturing for her to go away, so Flora shut her truck down and slipped out of the driver's seat, keeping her phone in her hand.

"Hi, Natalie," she said with forced cheer. "How are you doing?"

She glanced over at Kaylin, hoping Natalie would get the message—that she was here because of Kaylin.

"Thanks for coming, Flora," Natalie said. "You're just in time." She turned to Kaylin, her gaze narrowing. "I'm sorry, but as you can see, I have guests. I don't have time for this right now. Please, get off my property and don't come back."

Flora walked up the stairs and onto the porch, glad she had made the right decision. Kaylin glanced at Flora dismissively, then scoffed.

"I don't care what else you're doing right now. Spencer loved me. I know there are things he wanted me to have. Just let me in."

"I am not," Natalie said, ice in her voice, "letting you in to poke through my husband's things. Not in *my* house."

"It sounds like she wants you to leave," Flora said. She knew she wasn't exactly the most intimidating person, so she just hoped that the two of them combined would convince Kaylin to give it up. "Do you want me to call the police, Natalie?"

Natalie hesitated, and Kaylin took advantage of her indecision to lunge for the door, slam it open, and hurry into the house as if she owned the place—only to come to an abrupt stop as she slammed into someone who was on their way out.

Kaylin stumbled back, blinking up at Cameron, who Flora guessed the black SUV belonged to. It seemed she hadn't needed to be here after all—Natalie's brother was visiting her.

"It's you," Cameron said, his face twisting into something hateful as he stared at Kaylin. "You stole my sister's husband from her. You're the reason she's so miserable right now."

CHAPTER TWELVE

Natalie's eyes went wide. "Are you the one who killed Spencer?" she snarled at Kaylin.

Not waiting for an answer, she lunged at the other woman, who shrieked. Flora stepped forward and grabbed Natalie's arm, pulling her back. She had suspected as much herself, but she'd never had any proof. How did Cameron know? Was he working with the police? Why would they tell him something they hadn't told Natalie?

But then Cameron said, "That's not what I meant. You lost your husband a long time before he took his last breaths, Natalie. Because of her." He pointed right at Kaylin's face, and the other woman backed away from him. "I can't believe you have the gall to show your face here. Do you have any idea how much you hurt my sister?"

"I—I didn't even know he was married when I met him," Kaylin stammered. "By the time he told me, I was already in love with him. It's not my fault, it's his."

"Trust me, I lay just as much blame on him. But he's not here anymore, and you are. And I don't let anyone hurt my little sister."

His voice and his expression were dark and intense. Even though they weren't directed at her, Flora shivered. He sounded … he sounded like he was willing to kill.

Her fingers tightened on Natalie's arm as the thought occurred to her. Cameron had been picking up garbage the day of the murder, and hadn't Beth said that some of her friends who lived farther down the road were complaining that trash pickup had been late that day? It had been a normal day, up until that gunshot rang out, which meant Natalie had been at work, so Cameron wouldn't have been delayed while he was talking to her.

It was garbage pickup day, so no one would have thought twice about seeing a garbage truck drive by. And there weren't very many houses along the road. In fact, no other houses were visible from here. Cameron could easily have driven just a bit further up the road, out of sight of the house, and then come back on foot, carrying a gun, after he saw Spencer standing in the yard. There was no question that he was protective of his little sister, and he had known about the affair.

She had no idea whether he even owned a gun, but it seemed like almost everyone did out here in the middle of nowhere. She stepped farther back, pulling Natalie with her.

"Let go of me," the other woman said. "I put up with this for long enough. I hate her. I hate her so much."

"You don't want blood on your hands, Natalie," Cameron said with frightening calmness. He crossed his arms, looking down at Kaylin like she was a bug. "The last thing you need is trouble with the police right now. Let her go. I'm sure she'll get what's coming to her soon enough."

Kaylin paled and turned, running past Flora and Natalie and down the porch steps to her car. She pulled away with a screech of tires, nearly hitting Flora's truck as she backed out. Cameron just chuckled, then stepped out of the house onto the porch, jiggling his keys in his hand. "Sorry to run, Natalie, but I've got to go into town. You'll take care of her, won't you?"

This last question was directed toward Flora. She held his gaze, and whatever he read in her face made him frown.

"Don't go," Natalie said, pulling her arm away from Flora. "Please, Cameron. I'm upset. I don't want to be left alone."

"You won't be alone. You'll have your friend with you."

"She's not my friend!" Natalie snapped. She spared Flora a slightly apologetic look, but continued, "She's just my neighbor. I barely know her. Why do you have to leave? You were planning on staying all afternoon. And after Kaylin showed up... What if she returns?"

"She won't," Cameron said with certainty. "I'll make sure of it. You don't have to worry about anything." He stooped to kiss her cheek, then straightened up.

"I'll take care of it, just like I always do. No one is going to get away with hurting my little sister."

Flora grit her teeth, keeping her mouth shut. As soon as he pulled out of the driveway, she was going to call the police. She didn't know if she had enough proof to convince anyone of her suspicions, but she would do what it took to make sure someone found Kaylin and kept her safe, at least until the police had the chance to talk to Cameron.

Natalie didn't reply. She just stared at her brother, her eyes blank. Then her lips began to quiver. "Cameron? What did you do?"

Flora could hear the horrible suspicion in the woman's voice. She darted a glance at her truck, but she couldn't make a run for it, not with Natalie still here.

"I don't know what you're talking about," Cameron said with a fake smile. "Just hold tight, Natalie. This will all be over soon."

"No, wait," Natalie said, reaching out to grab his hand as he turned to go. "What are you going to do, Cameron?"

"Maybe you should leave," Cameron ground out, glancing at Flora. She hesitated but shook her head.

"I might not be Natalie's friend, but I'm not going anywhere."

"You don't trust me around my own sister?"

Flora didn't answer that, but that was answer enough for him. He pushed Natalie away gently and grabbed Flora's arm tight enough to make her yelp. "Listen, whatever you think you know, you're wrong. You need to keep your mouth shut; you got it?"

"What are you doing, Cameron?" Natalie said, pulling at his grip on Flora's arm. "Let her go. You're hurting her."

"I'm not hurting her," Cameron said. "Not yet. I like Flora. She's nice, and she always has a cold drink for me when I come to pick up the garbage. She's friends with Grady. I don't want to have to hurt her."

The warning in those words made Flora blanche. She tried to speak up, to say something that would convince him to let her go. But the words wouldn't come, and Natalie was the one who interceded again.

"You're scaring me. Cameron, did you … did you do something to Spencer? Are you the one who hurt him?"

The other woman's voice broke, and Cameron finally let go of Flora's arm. She stumbled back, rubbing at it and wondering if it would bruise.

"Whatever I did, or didn't do, I did for you, Natalie. You're my little sister. It's always been my job to protect you."

Natalie took in a shuddering breath, her eyes horrified. "Cameron, I loved him. What did you do? Please tell me you didn't kill him."

"He was hurting you," Cameron said. "I know he didn't stop the affair, Natalie. He was never going to stop. You were just going to get your heart broken again and again. And when I drove past that day, he had the gall to smile and wave at me, as if he had nothing to hide. I know you cared for him, but you'll be better off without him. You'll see."

"No," Natalie said, pulling away from him. "You *killed* him, Cameron. I know you don't understand, but I loved him."

"Maybe we should go inside," Flora murmured, putting a hand on the other woman's elbow.

Without warning, Cameron grabbed her arm again, dragging her off the porch. Flora stumbled on the steps and nearly went to her knees, but the man kept dragging her toward his SUV.

"I trust my sister not to say anything," he snapped, "but I don't trust you to keep your mouth shut. I'm sorry, Flora, I really did like you. I'll have to buy Grady a couple of drinks after this. I'm sure he'll be sad." He turned back to Natalie. "I'll come back this evening. I'll take care of everything. Don't worry."

Natalie stared after them, her face frozen with shock, but just as Cameron reached the SUV, she ran off the porch. Flora was trying to pull her arm away from the man, but his grip was like iron. He was strong—his job must have been a good daily workout.

"Cameron, stop it!" Natalie said. She grabbed Flora's other arm and tried to help her pull away, but his grip didn't falter. "You can't hurt her."

"You just said she's not your friend," Cameron snapped. "I'm not going to let her tell the police what you figured out. Just let it go, Natalie. None of this will affect you."

"What are you going to do to her?" Natalie asked. "You're going to hurt her, aren't you?"

"It doesn't concern you," Cameron snapped. "Leave it, Nat."

To Flora's horror, Natalie let go of her arm. Cameron took advantage to tug her forward roughly. He opened the back of the SUV, and Flora realized he was planning on taking her away to do ... whatever he was going to do to her.

"No," Natalie said. Her voice was shaking, but she managed to sound resolved regardless. "I'm going to call the police, Cameron. This isn't right. I can't... I can't let you hurt people."

Cameron was surprised enough that he loosened his grip on Flora's arm. She wrenched away from him and stumbled back, out of his reach. She had dropped her cell phone when he grabbed her and now, she glanced at the porch. It was right there, lying on the bottom step. She began backing toward it, keeping her eye on the siblings.

"You wouldn't do that," Cameron said, but he sounded uncertain.

Natalie took a deep breath. "I would. I *will*. This isn't you, something's wrong. You can't just ... you can't just kill people. That's not the brother I grew up with."

Flora crouched, not taking her eyes off of him, and grabbed her cell phone. She glanced down just long enough to bring up the phone app and dial 911. The two siblings were too focused on each other to pay any attention to her. She hesitated a second longer, but despite how upset Cameron was, it didn't look like he was threatening his sister. Instead, he seemed to be pleading with her. Slowly, Flora crept up the porch steps and through the house's open door. Once she was inside, she pushed it shut, turning the deadbolt.

Then, she lifted her phone to her ear. She just hoped the police could get here quickly, because she was shaking too much to be confident she could run away if Cameron decided to finish what he had started.

EPILOGUE

"That sweet boy?" Beth asked, putting her cup of tea down. They were sitting in Beth's kitchen. Tim was outside, doing yard work, and the older woman glanced out the window occasionally to make sure he was all right. Most of her attention, however, was focused on Flora. "I don't believe it."

"It was him," Flora said grimly. She rubbed her arm, which had bruised where he grabbed it. "Seriously. I barely got away with my life. I'm pretty sure he was planning on killing me."

"Oh, my," Beth said, pressing a hand to her lips. "I never even suspected... Are you all right? That must have been terrifying."

"It was," she said, not embarrassed to admit it. "I really thought I was going to die. But Natalie defended me, and I managed to get away. He took off in his SUV, but the police caught him. I just hope he doesn't get out of jail somehow. He'll probably come after me or Kaylin if he does."

"Poor Natalie," Beth mused. "I know it's not right to compare what she's going through to what happened with you, but she lost two of the most important men in her life in the span of a week. I feel terrible for her."

"Yeah." Flora grimaced. "I don't think she likes me any more now than she did before, but I've got a lot of respect for her. She stood up to her brother when it mattered, even though it's obvious the two of them were close. I owe her my life."

"You think you know someone." Beth shook her head. "It makes me wonder how many of the people in my life are hiding such terrible secrets. I hope you have friends and family you can trust, Flora."

"I do," she said, thinking of Violet, who had insisted on giving her a week's worth of free lattes when she heard what happened, and who had come over for a sleepover on the pullout couch the first night after the incident. She thought of Grady, who had pulled her in for an unexpected hug when he saw the bruises on her arm, and Sydney, who had snuck a few extra treats for Amaretto into her bag when she stopped by the feed store to stock up on canned food. Even though she was still shaken by the whole experience, they were making her feel safe. And now she was here with Beth, a woman she didn't always like, but whom she trusted. A friend, no matter how different the two of them were.

"And you know, if you ever need anything…"

Flora smiled and sipped her tea. "I know. I can come to you."

Made in the USA
Coppell, TX
15 November 2023